PRAISE FOR MEG GREHAN'S *THE DEEPEST BREATH*

A *Bank Street* Best Children's Book of 2022
with Outstanding Merit

A *Booklist* 2021 Editor's Choice

Winner: Judges' Special Award,
KPMG Children's Books Ireland Awards 2021

Shortlisted: Waterstones Children's Book Prize 2020

"Heartwarming and tear-provoking"
Booklist, starred review

"Wholesome, powerful and essential"
Shelf Awareness, starred review

"I spent most of this beautifully written verse novel blinking back tears ... I felt genuinely distraught to have finished it."
Sarah Webb, *The Irish Independent*

PRAISE FOR MEG GREHAN'S *THE LONELY BOOK*

Nominated: Yoto Carnegie Medal for Writing 2024

"This brave, kind novel in verse explores gender identity in an original way."
Sarah Webb, *The Irish Independent*

"What a tender jewel of a book ... *The Lonely Book* was a balm and a blessing."
Deirdre Sullivan, author of *Savage Her Reply*

PRAISE FOR MEG GREHAN'S *BABY TEETH*

A *Kirkus* YA Book of the Year 2022
Shortlisted: An Post Irish Book Awards 2021
Nominated: Carnegie Medal 2023

"Emotionally rich and gloriously queer"
Kirkus, starred review

"An excellent addition to LGBTQIA+ and verse novel collections."
School Library Journal

"Skillfully charts uncertainty, temptation and the course of a strange, desperate love."
Imogen Russell Williams, *The Guardian*

MEG GREHAN

The Brightest Star

THE BRIGHTEST STAR

First published in 2025 by
Little Island Books, New Work Junction,
11 Wynnefield Road, Rathmines, Dublin, Ireland, D06 F9C1
First published in the USA in 2025

Text © Meg Grehan 2025
Illustrations © Nene Lonergan 2025

The author has asserted her moral rights.

All rights reserved. No part of this book may be reproduced,
transmitted or stored in a retrieval system in any form or by any means
(including electronic/digital, mechanical, photocopying, scanning,
recording or otherwise, by means now known or hereinafter invented)
without prior permission in writing from the publisher.

Product safety queries can be addressed to Little Island Books
at the above address or info@littleisland.ie

A British Library Cataloguing in Publication record for this book is
available from the British Library.

Cover illustrations by Nene Lonergan
Cover layout by Ali Ardington
Typesetting by Rosa Devine
Proofread by Isabel Dwyer
Printed in England by CPI

Paperback ISBN: 978-1-915071-80-4
US Hardback ISBN: 978-1-915071-91-0
Ebook ISBN: 978-1-915071-97-2

Little Island has received funding to support this book from the Arts
Council of Ireland / An Chomhairle Ealaíon

10 9 8 7 6 5 4 3 2 1

To Cheyenne, Ella, Barry, Olivia, Aria, Ashley and everyone at Treehouse Shakers.

Thank you for understanding, transforming and sharing *The Deepest Breath* so beautifully.

This book wouldn't exist without you.

I know a lot of things
About a lot of things
But the thing I know the most about
Is me
Stevie

I know that I am exactly twelve years and 364 days old
I know it's my birthday tomorrow
And that my hair is still brown
My eyes are still green
And I'm still allergic to peanuts

I know I have a mum
Whose room is right next to mine
And sometimes
At night
We tap and scratch Morse code messages to each other
Morse code is great for telling jokes
I know that

I know I have a dad
Who I haven't talked to in a while
And I know that that's OK
And definitely not my fault
I still hope he sends a birthday card
Though I know
He won't

I know I love space and stars and the possibility
    of aliens
I know what I think happened to Anastasia
And I know I love tea with two sugars
I know that the ocean isn't really all that scary
And octopuses are still very cool

I know I get this feeling
When I look at my best friend
Chloe
I know it's fizzy and warm and lovely and
I know
Exactly
What it is

I know I want to hold her hand
And maybe kiss her some day
And I want us to grow up together
And I know
Exactly
What this feeling is
When I look at Chloe
I feel
Affection
I feel bravery
I feel
Pride

I know a lot about me
But I also know a lot about Chloe
I know she is kind and cool and funny
I know she is way better at maths than I am
And that she helps me when I get stuck
Because she is a very good best friend
I know that
I know she still paints her nails every week
Pink this week!
And she still loves magic
And is somehow
Still
Confusing me
With it
Which is sometimes frustrating
Because I like to know how things work
But it's also very
Very
Impressive

I think Chloe is the coolest
I love when we hang out
When we read together
When we go to the aquarium
Our favourite place
Together

We have a teddy we share
His name is Sydney
And he's an octopus
My very favourite octopus
We take turns minding him and sometimes
We bring him to the aquarium
With us
It's our own
Special thing

We have another best friend
His name is Andrew
And he has moved
From the very best cookies
To the very best, most delicious, most elaborate
Cakes
He's making my birthday cake
And that makes me feel
Special
And loved
And known
Because he said he's going to make it
Space themed!

I love space
I know it seems scary
I do
So big
So vast
So

So
Unknown
But I think that's what I like about it
I can't possibly know everything about space
Nobody does!
But I can learn
And explore
And wonder
And that feels
Freeing
And exciting

The sea used to scare me
So I wrote about it in my notebook
My notebook is giant
It has hundreds of pages
And I still
Still!
Haven't used them all
But I think that's a good thing
Because before
When I was scared
I would use my notebook to make me feel safe
I would collect information
Facts and figures and findings
And I would store them all
In this book
Just
In
Case

In case of what?
I'm not sure
You see
I thought
That if I knew everything there was to know
    in the world
I would be ready for anything
I would be safe safe safe
But here's the thing!
I am safe
I might still feel scared
I might still feel anxious
But I don't feel
Unsafe
Any more
Because
Because!
I trust myself

And I know I have my mum
And she's the grown-up
(even if I'm about to be thirteen)
And I know I can go to her if anything
Scares me
Or worries me
I know now
That not all bad things
Are big bad things
I know that
And I trust myself to know the difference

I know I have Chloe and Andrew
And I can turn to them
Any time I have a problem
Or need some help or advice

And I know I have Dr Wells
My therapist
Who reminds me
Every week
That I am strong
That I am brave
That I am capable and worthy and wonderful
Though
Honestly
I don't think I need reminding
Any more
Because now
I think
That's something
I know
Too

I wake on the day of my birthday
Very aware
That it's my birthday
I'm excited
But there are nerves sitting heavy in my stomach

I've invited people from my class
Including Chloe and Andrew
Of course
And my cousins

I wish I'd just invited Chloe and Andrew
I wish it was just going to be the three of us
And Andrew's cake

But Mum insisted
And it seemed like the right thing to do
She said it was special
That I'd only turn thirteen once
Which seems irrelevant to me
Because I'll only be every age once
What makes thirteen so special?

Well
OK
I know what makes it special for me

It means that next week
I start secondary school
It means a little more
                Freedom
A few less rules maybe
New friends maybe
Not that I need them
Exactly
New things to learn
New teachers to meet
New clubs to join
Maybe
Maybe
A new me
Maybe

It's not that I don't like me
Of course not
I remind myself all the time
That I am great
Exactly as I am
But it would be nice if
Maybe
Maybe
No one knew about my anxiety
Like everyone in my class now does
If they didn't know how scared I
   used to be
New people means a new opportunity

To be brave
To be seen as brave
I want to be seen as brave
I do
I don't know why
It matters so much
But it feels
Important

Mum makes me a giant hot chocolate
With a flake and everything
And there's a giant present lying on the kitchen table
Wrapped beautifully
As always
And my fingers itch to unwrap it
But I am thirteen now
So I show some
Restraint
Though I can barely focus on what my mum is telling me
And eventually
She just laughs
And says
Oh OK!
Just open it!

And I do
And I send the paper flying

I am not a neat unwrapper
I do not carefully remove the tape and fold up the paper
No no no
I tear that paper to shreds and when I've torn it all
Sitting in front of me
Is something
So beautiful
Something so
So perfect
That I start to tear up a little

A telescope
A real
Proper
Telescope
Sits in front of me
And
Maybe it's silly
But I whisper
Is it mine?
Because
Could it possibly
Be mine?
Am I deserving of something so wonderful?
And Mum tears up too
Like she knows what I'm thinking
And she takes my hand

And she looks at it
My fingers tangled with hers
And I know she's thinking about how
It used to be so small
And suddenly
I feel so
Big
And it feels
Strange
So I hug her
To feel small
And it works
She wraps her arms around me
Envelops me
Pulls me close close closer
and I feel safe again
Even though I know I wasn't ever unsafe
I know that I do I do

After a minute
We look back to the telescope
And Mum whispers
Of course it's yours
You deserve it
I hope you love it
I hope you enjoy it
I hope you don't spot any aliens
And oh!
I hope I do!

Soon guests start arriving
And all I want to do
Is show Chloe and Andrew my telescope
I just want the day to hurry up and be over
So night will come
And we can look at the stars together
And learn about constellations
And search for UFOs

But I have to put my telescope in my room
With a promise to come back later
And go downstairs

People in my class
Kind of
Know Chloe and I
Like each other
    Like
    Like like
        each other
At least
I think they do
We are very close
And I think a little obvious
But I can't be
Sure
Sometimes
Though
They make fun

Just a little
But mostly
They're nice

Only the nicest are here today
I think maybe the nicest thing for me to do
Would have been to invite
Everyone
But the idea of
Everyone
In my house
All at once
Gives me that anxious feeling in my chest
And my tummy and
No
I don't want that
So I explained to my mum
And my teacher
And my therapist
That it would just be too
Overwhelming
And they understood
So we
Compromised
And invited eight people from my class
Which still feels like a lot to me
But
Mum says
It's a party
Parties need people

And when everyone has arrived
Everyone from school
My best best friends
My cousins and their parents
I look at my mum
And she looks so
Happy
And she looks at me
And she looks so
Proud
And I decide
To try my best
To just
Have
Fun
And I do
You know
I do!
I have fun
I try to talk to everyone
To spend time with everyone
But soon
Everyone has formed their own little groups
And I'm free to wander back over to where
   Andrew and Chloe
Are in a very
Heated
Debate

Andrew and Chloe
Are always
In a debate
Sometimes heated
Sometimes cold
Sometimes light
Sometimes heavy
Sometimes they go on for days
Sometimes minutes
Sometimes Andrew wins
Sometimes Chloe wins
Sometimes no one wins
But always
No matter what
I am stuck in the middle

Not today
I decide
It is my birthday
My day
I decide
Though part of me hates
Thinking that

So I bounce up to them
With a happy
Hi guys!
And they say
A distracted hi

And a distracted hey
And get right back to it
I sigh
And plop down next to them
To listen
To be with them
To try
Not to get involved
But the topic
The topic
Draws me in

Of course there are aliens
Chloe nearly yells
Of course there aren't
Andrew does yell
And Chloe
Being Chloe
Whips out her best facts

Ever since I taught Chloe about fish
She has loved learning things
Just like me
We spend hours researching together
We pass notes with new facts we've learned
She still won't share how she does that thing
    with the magic cards
But she shares
Everything else

We know so much
And I love that we share that knowledge
We share facts about fish and history and
    geography and nature and animals and
    books and
And and and
All sorts
We share it all
And I love
That it isn't just mine
Any more
This thirst, this hunger, this drive
This knowledge
I love that it
Is ours

The Milky Way
Chloe begins
Has somewhere between
One hundred
And four hundred
Billion
Stars
In it
And
And!
It's not the only galaxy out there
It's one of
At least

At least!
Two
Trillion
Galaxies
And you
Andrew
You
Want me
Want us
To believe
That we're the only life?
The only things living
In all of space
In all
That
space
And suddenly
Though I already knew this
In theory
Something about the way
Chloe says it
Makes me so aware
That space
Space is
Scary
It's big and it's unknown and there's no air and no gravity and I thought
I thought aliens would be cool
In theory

In theory!
And my chest does that thing
But I tell myself
Self
No
You are here
On earth
Feet on the ground
Hands on the ground
You are here and you are real and that is
   all that matters
Space is up there
And it is big
And it is unknown
And it is scary
But you are safe and you are OK and you are
Here
And I breathe and I breathe and I breathe
And I am OK

OK
Andrew challenges
But there's no proof of
Anything
Yet
And most planets we know of
Seem entirely
Uninhabitable

So
Why would I waste my time and my brain cells
Believing in something
That by all accounts so far
Just does not
Exist

But maybe it does
Chloe says
Or maybe it will
Or maybe
It did
She says sadly
Maybe we're the only ones left
Maybe

And I am suddenly
Immeasurably
Sad
I worry about the climate a lot
But I do my part
And I try my best
To have as positive an impact as I can have on this planet
So does Mum
So do my friends
We learn about it in school and it's scary
Our planet is precious
And we need to protect it

The idea of other planets...
I shake my head
It's just something Chloe said to win the debate
It's just something
Chloe said
To win
The debate

Well that's just ridiculous
Andrew snaps
Think about Mars
For example
The Viking missions sent to
Find signs of life
Found no evidence of microbial life!
No organic molecules in the soil!
No organic molecules
No life!
He ends triumphantly

And
Chloe asks
Crossing her arms
When were those missions
Exactly?

Andrew pales
Well that's beside the point
He mutters

1976! Chloe yells
Throwing her hands in the air
I win!
I win I win I win!

Well
Hang on
Andrew tries again
That doesn't mean their findings were wrong

No Chloe concedes
But the fact that the rover
Curiosity
Has found organic molecules
Several
Several!
Times
And that recent missions
Have found proof of water
Water!
Does prove them wrong!

Andrew pales a little more
Well
He says
I guess I haven't got that far in the book yet
And Chloe laughs
Big and loud and hearty
And Andrew

Giggles a little
And blushes
Then he's laughing too
Big and loud and hearty
And everything is good again
And I can breathe and relax and enjoy the party
With my best friends

When everyone has gone home
At last at last at last
Everyone except Chloe and Andrew
Of course of course of course
We sit around the kitchen table
Eating second helpings of Andrew's cake
Which was
Incredible
By the way
The icing looked like a galaxy
All blue and purple with tiny stars
And there was a little icing alien
Sitting on top
Holding a book
And looking in wonder at the sky
And I love them
That little alien
I love them
And I refuse to let anyone eat them

We talk about my new telescope
And all the things we're going to see
When we can tear ourselves away from the cake
And go upstairs to set it up
When we go upstairs
They both sit on the bed
And watch

As I
Slowly slowly
Open the box
And oh
It's beautiful
And for a moment I even wish
Chloe and Andrew weren't here
So I could have a little cry
And gaze at the stars and just
Feel thankful
Then I remember
That they love me
And I do those things anyway

The sky is so
So astounding
Like Chloe said
There are
                    At least
A hundred billion stars
In our galaxy
The stars swirl in a pinwheel pattern
And make up the Milky Way
We live pretty far out
About two-thirds of the way out
On one of the arms of the pinwheel

I wonder how many stars I'll be able to see
I try to remember all the constellations
My dad taught me

But I've forgotten loads
I decide I must learn them again
This time I don't need my dad to teach me them
Though
I'll do it by myself
It takes a while to figure out how to use the telescope
But eventually
We see
Stars
We even see
A shooting star
And in that moment
With my friends beside me
I'm so happy
I don't even know
What to wish for

I did wish on my birthday candles though
I did
I closed my eyes tight
And I blew out the candles
And I wished and wished and wished
That next week
At my new school
Everything will be
OK
I wished that Mum wouldn't worry too much
That Chloe and Andrew would stay by my side
That I'd learn new and interesting things

That I might even make
Some new friends
I know it's a lot for one cake
But I figure
Thirteen candles
Can handle a big wish
Did you know
That once or twice
In every fifteen or so years
Mars
Is close enough for us to see from earth
That means
I think
That if there's any life up there
It's close enough for them
To see us too
And I know
That if there's life up there
It's most likely just
Little
Tiny
Molecules
Who don't know or care about
Us
Here
On earth
But I care about them

When my friends have gone home
And Mum has said goodnight
And it's just me and my telescope
I look up at the sky
To where I think
Though I don't really know
To where I think
Mars might be
And I say
Hello
Quietly
Just a little
Hello
A whisper sent out into space

The next day
I can't wait for it to get dark
But I still enjoy the day
Mum and I go school supply shopping
And I get new pens
Which I love
And highlighters
Which I love even more
And some notebooks
Don't even get me started
On notebooks

We go for hot chocolate together
And we talk about my birthday
And how it went
And how different thirteen feels
To twelve
After a little while
She asks about Chloe
So
She says
How's it going
And I blush
And say we're just friends
Though that isn't entirely true
It isn't untrue
But it isn't the whole truth
When it comes to Chloe and me
We are
Something
We are
More
And I'm not sure exactly what we are
But we are
Something
Good

Something I want to hold
Like I sometimes hold her hand
Something I want to keep
Like I keep Sydney beside my bed

(on my weeks, anyway)
We are something
Something
Something
Good

OK Mum says
Saving me from my blush
Just know
And don't forget
That you can talk to me
About Chloe
About anything
Anything at all
Any time
And I thank her
And say Chloe and I are good
We are so good
And I still like her
But I don't feel ready to do anything with that
    like yet
And she feels the same
So
We are friends
Special friends
And it is nice
And it is sweet
And it is lovely
And it makes me

Happy
Happy
Happy

Then my mum says something that surprises me
She looks into my eyes
And she says
Just don't forget about
Andrew
OK

And I don't know what to do with that
So I just say
OK

Have I forgotten Andrew?
I spend most days with him and Chloe
And I talk to him all the time
And I guess we haven't baked together in a while
But that's just because we're busy
Busy with
Chloe
And oh
I guess I haven't spent time with only Andrew
In a while
But I don't think he minds
Surely
Surely not
Maybe
I think

I'll invite only Andrew over
For some baking
And cooking shows
But then I imagine
Chloe's face
Her disappointment
At being left out
And I just
Can't
I spend time alone with Chloe
I do
So why is it different?
I'm not sure
I'm not
Sure
At home I try on my new uniform
A blue plaid skirt
A little too long
A blue jumper
A little too baggy
White shirt
Blue socks
Black shoes

It's all
A little
Big
Well
Mum says
Room to grow!

And I nod and smile
And hope
I don't look
Silly

Chloe
I ask the next day
Is your uniform—
Miles too big?
She interrupts
Yes
Absolutely
Mum says I'll—
Grow into it
We say together
And laugh
And I feel
So much
Better

The last few days of summer holidays
Fly by
I read
I look at the stars through my telescope
I jot down notes
I learn and I learn
And then
When the next Monday comes
I feel ready
To learn
Even more

Mum and I spend lots of time together
Over those last few days
We cook nice dinners together and we
Watch old movies
We do the annual
Big Clean
Before school starts
We even rearrange my room
To signify
My new beginning

My room is small
But it is perfect
It is cosy and warm and full of things I love
My books
My plushies

And now
My telescope
We clear everything away from the window
So there's plenty of room for stargazing
We arrange some notebooks on the windowsill
And a mug full of pens
So I can log my findings
Quickly and easily
We stack up my books about space
So I can reference them
Quickly and easily
And I look at my mum
Heaving stacks of books around
Sweaty from pushing my bed around
Until we found the perfect place
For it
I look at her
And I am filled
With love
With gratitude
With
With
Adoration
I feel so lucky
To have a mum
Who knows what I need
Before I do
Who takes my interests
So seriously
That she pushes all my furniture aside

Just so I have more room to
Do what I love to do
Who listens to me talk about the stars
And planets and aliens and how I'm becoming more
And more convinced
They're real
And she never judges me
For how my interests jump around
Or for how
Consumed I become with them
She just learns with me
And sometimes
She says thank you
For teaching me something new
And when she says that
My heart soars
Because
I have someone
Who I know
Cares and cares and cares
And I feel
Lucky and lucky and lucky

That night
Two nights before school starts
I can't sleep
I consider writing a letter to Chloe
Because that's something we've started doing
Like people in

The olden times
But I don't know what to say
Dear Chloe
I'm honestly a little...
Dear Chloe
I'm worried that I've...
Dear Chloe
Do you think...
No
Everything in my head
Seems stuck there
Even though
I thought
I'd become quite good
At sharing what worries me
But I haven't told anyone
That I'm worried
I'm worried about school
That I won't be smart enough
That I won't be
Cool
Enough
I'm worried my friends
Will find new friends
And won't need me any more
I'm even worried
About life on Mars
Ever since
Chloe and Andrew's debate
My worries

Used to
At least
Be limited to
One planet
I don't like to be worried
I thought I was past this
I thought I had
Grown
But maybe
I am still
Just a little kid
Full of worries
And maybe
There's nothing I can do
About that
But then
I remember everything
I've learned
I remember that when I first met
Dr Wells
She said
You like learning
Don't you?
And I said Yes
Very much
And she said
Well do you know
What the number one
Most important

Thing we can learn about is?
And I shook my head
And she pointed at her chest
And said
Ourselves
You
Stevie
You are the thing you should most want
  to learn about
And I imagine
You'll enjoy it
Because you
Are interesting and kind and smart
And so many more things
And once you learn all those other things
You'll only feel
More strong and solid and secure
So
What do you say?
And I thought about it
About how I'd just learned something new
  about myself
That I like girls
Like like girls
That is
And I thought about how
Once that made sense to me
I did feel stronger and more solid and more
  secure

And then
Suddenly
I felt so
Excited
To see what else I could learn about myself
And extra excited
That I have
My whole life to learn it
All

And remembering this
What she said
And how I felt
I decide
To try to worry
A little less
Because of all the things I've learned about myself
How brave I am
How capable I am and
How strong I am
Are some of my favourites
I still can't sleep though
Now I'm kind of buzzing
I have the worry still in my tummy
But I'm working on it
I write it all down
And decide to share it with my mum the next day
But I'm still wide awake

And excited to learn again
So I go to my telescope
And I decide
However silly it may sound
                I don't care
To look for UFOs
Just in case
And I imagine
A little spaceship
Flying high above me
With a little alien inside
Looking down
And I figure
If I can't tell my mum right now
Maybe
I'll tell them
So I stay up another hour
Peering through my telescope
And whispering all my worries and secrets
And when they're all out
I sleep

It's the last day before school
And Mum is
Buzzing
About the house
Checking I have everything I need
Checking my uniform is clean
Though I don't know how it would've gotten dirty
Then
When the Big Clean is completely finished
And the house is gleaming
And my bag is packed
And my uniform is hanging on my wardrobe door
We sit
And we do my favourite thing we do together
We read
I'm reading a book Susan
The librarian
Helped me pick out
I told her I like space now
Really really like space
And she found a book about a rover
Exploring Mars
I love it
But the rover is so lonely
My mum is reading a book about space too
Susan and I chose it for her
I chose a little selfishly

Because it looks like one I would like to read
But it's huge and the text is tiny
And it looks
Intimidating
So I gave it to my mum
Hoping she would read it and tell me
All the most interesting
Bits
And I was right
In my hope
Because not only is my mum reading the book
But she's taking
Notes
For me
And sometimes she turns to me
All excited
And absolutely
Bursts
Stevie!
Did you know!
Stevie!
Did you know
Stevie!
And so far
I haven't known
But now
Thanks to my mum
And her enthusiasm
And her love
And her sharing

I do

That night
I can't sleep
Again
So I go to my telescope
And I tell the aliens
I haven't found yet
That I'm scared
That I'm nervous
That I'm
That maybe I'm
That I'm
Not ready
For big school
Secondary school
More people
Bigger building
More teachers
New people
New place
And I'm still me
And everyone
Mum and Chloe and Andrew keep saying
Oh!
New beginning new beginning new beginning
Like everything will change and everything will
    be better
And we will change and we will be better
And I don't know that it will

And I don't know that I will
And I don't know that I want to
I don't know that I
Want to

I am up early
After only getting
A few hours of sleep
I am ready to go
Tea made
Cereal poured
When Mum comes downstairs

Look at you!
She squeals
Looking at me with so much pride
And even though I feel a little ridiculous
In my too big uniform
I give her my biggest smile
And a big
Thumbs up
For some reason
I am tired

We pull up to the school
And I see Chloe waiting by the gate
Reading the newest book in her favourite series
Which is about witches and princesses and
    unicorns
And seeing her with that familiar book
From that familiar series

Makes me feel better
Chloe is still Chloe
Not everything
Is changing
Not really
No

So I give my mum a hug
And lug my gigantic backpack
Out of the car
And dash
As quickly as I can with all my books on my back
Over to Chloe

She smiles at me
And my heart
Jumps
And I wonder if that will
Ever
Stop
And I decide
I hope
It doesn't

We wait for Andrew and I tell her one of my
New most interesting facts about space
Thanks Mum!
Did you know one million earths could fit inside
   the sun?

She didn't
And she lights up with how interesting my new
    interesting fact is
And I feel bright and warm

When Andrew arrives
The three of us
Take a moment
And just
Look at each other
And I think of the last almost-two-years
Of the three of us
Being best friends
And I cross my fingers
In my pocket
That nothing
Nothing at all
Changes

We smile at each other
We each let a little nervous laugh out
And we head in
Through the big gates
Into the big building
Into the big
Crowd
And I'm nervous
I am
But I'm excited
I am

I am
I am

We go to a big hall
And we sit amongst
At least a hundred other students
All of us in our blue uniforms
With our giant bags
And our various levels of anxiety
Written on our faces
I look around
And I realise I'm not the only one who's nervous
We three
Aren't the only ones
And I don't know how
That makes me feel
Better or worse
Or something
Else

We're sorted into our class groups and
Only Andrew and I are together
In class One-S
Chloe is in One-L
And I feel a pang
A pang of sadness
To lose Chloe
Of panic
To be without her in this new world

A pang of relief
To have Andrew
A pang of excitement
To start learning
A pang of anxiety
Looking round at all the
Unfamiliar faces

After we're sorted into our classes
And told all about the school and the rules and the traditions
We're led to our new classrooms
For first year
We have a base classroom
Where we stay
And the teachers come to us
And I'm glad
Because this place
Seems gigantic to me
And I just know
I would get
Lost

I sit beside Andrew
And take out my notebook
And my pens
And my highlighters
And try to make myself
At home

Try to make myself
Comfortable
And Andrew takes out a notebook
And a single pen
And looks in awe
At my selection of colours
Why do you need all those?
He asks
For colour coding I say
Of course
We meet our class teacher
Who is the one we are to go to with any
Issues
We may
Have
We meet older students
Who are to show us around
And then
We meet some older kids
Who run
The groups
And clubs
In the school

There's the anime club
And the drama club
And the choir
And the orchestra
And then

Then
A kid who must be about sixteen
Who has amazing blue hair
Introduces themself
Hi
They say
I'm Nate
My pronouns are they/them
And I'm here to tell you about the LGBTQIA+ group here
And my heart
Lights up
And my tummy
Squiggles
In a good way
And my hands get clammy
In an excited way

An LGBTQIA+ group!
A group of people
Like me
A group of people
On journeys like mine
A group of people
With hearts
Like mine
I can't wait to tell Chloe
I look at Andrew
Filled up with the sparkling potential

This group's existence
Has brought
Me
I look at him
And he is staring at the desk in front of him
Eyes down
Face pinched
And I feel the excitement
Drain a little
Because something
Is wrong
With
Andrew

Nate tells us all about the group
And I try to just
Feel hopeful
And happy and excited
And try not to worry
Too much
About Andrew
Sitting stiffly beside me
Nate says anyone is welcome
Whether they're part of the community or not
All identities are accepted
And so long as you respect people's pronouns
And expression
And space
You are

More
Than
Welcome
I am more
Than
Welcome

When Nate leaves
Waving happily
I turn
Slowly
To Andrew
Hey
I say
Hey
He says
You OK?
I ask
Why?
He asks
You seem
Off
I say
No I don't
He says
OK
I murmur
OK
He murmurs

We go find Chloe
Chloe! I almost yell
Did you hear about the LGBTQIA+ club?
Yes!
She nearly yells back
We had a super cool girl named Marie
Tell us about it
She said she was bisexual
She just said it
All confident and proud
And it was so
So cool
And inspiring and
Wow
She says
Just
Wow
You know?
And I do
I know

Wow

Andrew is quiet all day
And Chloe is loud all day
They don't even debate once
About anything
Because Andrew is busy being quiet and
    mysterious and strange

And Chloe is busy being loud and exciting
    and herself
So so herself
She is alight with this new information
A club!
Of people like us!
Maybe
We could even
Tell them
That we like like each other
Maybe there
We could just be
Ourselves
Together

When I get home I tell my mum all about it
All about Nate and Marie and how lovely and
    open and proud they were
How I've never met a non-binary person before
But now I have
And they were so cool
And I told Mum all about their blue hair
And she told me not to get any ideas
That I can't dye my hair until I'm
At least
Fifteen
And I roll my eyes
And say
OK

But in my head
I'm picturing myself with purple hair
And I must admit
I look quite cool
Too

I don't tell Mum about Andrew
Not yet
I want her help
Her opinion
Her advice
But first
I just want to be excited
And happy
My first day is over!
And I did it!
I got through it
With no anxiety!
Plenty of nerves
Sure
But no big anxiety
No panic
No tears
No regrets
No bumps
No wobbles
Nothing
I just
Did it

And in more ways than one
Today
I am proud

So
OK
This notebook
Is for
Recipes
Usually
But Stevie uses hers
For learning about things she doesn't
Understand
And I seem to have a pretty big thing
That I don't understand

Me

I know I am Andrew
But I don't think I know
What that means
Not really
I think
If you were to ask
Someone else
They'd say
Oh
Andrew
Well
He's nice
Likes baking
A lot
Likes
His friends

A lot
Used
To
Like
Football
Wonder
What
Happened
There...
And I'd agree
I do like baking
I do like my friends
I did like football
Before
Well
Before

But there just
Must   be

More   to

Me   than

that
But when I try
To think of those
Things
I can only think of

Bad things

Oh

Andy

He's

Selfish

He's

Jealous

He's

Not as smart

Not as talented

Can't keep up

Oh
Andy

Oh
Him

You could get to know him
I guess

But what
Is
There
To
Know
Really?

Oh
Andy
Oh
Him

Andrew is still quiet the next day
Chloe and I spend lunch squealing
About how excited we are
For LGBTQIA+ club
Tomorrow
We look at everyone around us
With hope and curiosity
Wondering who we'll meet there
Who here
Could be
Our new
Friends

But Andrew
Is silent
Don't worry Andy
Chloe says
Suddenly
Allies are welcome too
You won't be left out
And he looks up at her
And his face
Is a strange mixture of emotions
Confusion and sadness and loneliness and
And hope
I think

What's an ally?
He asks
And Chloe jumps to tell him

An ally
She says grandly
Is a person who doesn't identify as LGBT+
But who supports people who do!
And Andrews face lights up
OK he says
Well
I guess
I can be that
And I smile at him
And he smiles at me
And I hope
That's the end
Of the strangeness
Between us
Of his silence
Of his sadness

For the rest of the day
Andrew is cheerier
He is lighter
He is
Brighter

And Chloe
Is happy happy

Happy
She is excited
She is thriving
She is talking to everyone
And showing them
Magic tricks
She has new friends
In her new class
And I am trying
My very best
To just be
Happy
For
Her
We go to my house after school
Do our homework together
And even though
We're tired
From the first two days of our new routines
We have fun
Chloe helps me with my maths
I help her with her science
Andrew finishes first
And bakes cookies
And the familiar smell
Warms me
And fills me
With joy and a sense of peace and comfort
And I am suddenly so
Happy

So grateful
That Andrew is my friend
Even though things were weird for a minute
I'm just thankful things are better now
That a little weirdness
Can't detangle our friendship
Even when so much around us is changing
Andrew is stubborn and impatient
And he is kind and sweet
He is fun and he is funny and he is smart and he is talented
And I am his friend
And I am very
Very happy
About that

Sometimes I think
I am just
~~Dumb~~
~~Silly~~
~~Stupid~~
Dramatic
Attention-seeking
Fake
That I make it all worse
In my head
Than it could ever be
In the real world
In real life
Sometimes I think
I think
Too much

Sometimes
In my head
I can be a little mean

Sometimes
In my head
I can be a little mean
To me

But
I make great cookies
And I laugh and smile a lot

And I do well at school
(Even if really
I think it's a little boring)
And everyone seems to think
I'm just
Fine
Good
Sorted

Oh you know

Andrew

Chloe stays a little later than Andrew
And we talk about
Tomorrow
About the Rainbow Club
Which we've learned it's called
And which we love
Love love love
How lucky we feel
To be part of a rainbow
To be part of something
So lovely
We sit on the sofa
And we put on a movie
And instead of watching
We are focused
So focused
On our hands
On how close they are to each other
On how they're getting
Closer
Inch by inch
Until
Wow
Our fingers tangle
And wow
Her hand is in mine
And wow
I feel
So warm

In a good way
In a nice way
In a
Sweet way
Warm and safe
Warm and safe
Warm and safe

I wake an hour later
And Chloe is looking at me
Hey
She says
My dad is here
I have to go
And I pout before I realise what I'm doing
And she laughs
And I laugh
And she lets go of my hand
And I hold it in my other hand
To keep her warmth there
Cling to the feeling of being held
I smile at her
And she smiles at me
And she says
Tomorrow!
And I say
Tomorrow!
And she leaves
And I feel

Lonely and excited and sleepy and
Ready
For another
Day

Rainbow Club is during lunch
And it's all I can think about during our morning
　classes
I'm buzzy beneath my skin
Fizzy and excited and ready

I meet Chloe in the hallway
And we hug and squeal a little
OK
Let's go
Let's go!
I hook my arm around hers and turn
To hook my other arm
Through Andy's
But Andrew
Isn't there

　　　　　　　　　I tried
　　　　　　　　　I tried
　　　　　　　　　I tried
　　　　　　　　　I tried

　　　　　　　　I couldn't
　　　　　　　　I couldn't
　　　　　　　　I couldn't
　　　　　　　　I couldn't

I can't I can't I can't I can't

　　　　　　　　I'm sorry

We look for him
Call his name
Run to the classroom
The canteen
The yard
He's nowhere to be found
And we don't want to be late
To Rainbow Club
We look at each other
And we grimace a little
And we nod a little
And we go

OK   fine

I'll talk about it

OK   fine
The club

OK

Fine

I saw the way
Her face
Lit up
And I saw the way
Chloe's did
Too and
OK
Fine
I got
J e a l o u s
And

Maybe

A

Little

Scared

Because

Because

because.

Rainbow Club
Is in a classroom
Covered in colour
There are flags and banners and bunting
Rainbows and
    Blue purple pink
        Yellow purple black
            White blue pink
They go on
They cover the walls
They hang from the ceiling
It feels like walking through a rainbow
Into a different world
Nate is there
And they wave and say hi
Gently but enthusiastically
We take our seats and we wait
And people come trickling in
People who look like they might be part
    of the club
With colourful hair and
Pins with bright colours
And people who don't
But who walk in just as bravely and confidently
People greet each other
They hug and jump and their excitement
Is contagious
Everyone just seems so
Happy

So confident
So comfortable
It feels like such
A safe place
A safe group of people
A safe space

We go round and introduce ourselves
Hi my name is Stevie
My pronouns are she/her
I'm in first year
I
Um
I
Like girls
A lot
And everyone says hi and welcome and smiles and nods and some even clap a little
Quietly and kindly
Just to say
Good for you
And I hear it
And I feel it
Good for you
Good for you
Stevie

Chloe introduces herself next
Hi! I'm Chloe!

I think my pronouns are
She/her
But to be honest
I didn't know I had
Other options
So that's exciting!
And she beams
And she glows
And she looks at me
And we beam
And we glow
Together

We talk about things we could do throughout the year
Fundraisers we might want to do
Charities we might want to support
Things we might want to explore
Talk about
Learn about
Places we might want to go
People we might want to talk to
The potential
In the air
Is so potent
So palpable
So delicious
I look at Chloe
I look at all these people
I already know

I have something in common with
I look down at my hands
And I am so
Aware
That I am real
That I am here
And I feel good
I feel safe
I feel
I feel
Like when I hold Chloe's hand

When I hold Chloe's hand
My skin tingles
And I feel
Like everything
Will be OK
When I hold Chloe's hand
My heart doesn't beat faster
Not like I thought it would
I thought I would be nervous and anxious and scared
And my heart would beat and beat and beat faster and faster and faster
But when she takes my hand
Or I take hers
My heart feels
Calm
And
Sure

Beat
Beat
Beat
Happy
Happy
Happy
Held held held
Had had had
And the only thing that can bother me
That can make me sad
Is the fact
That at some point
At some point
I'll have to let go

We don't hold hands during the club meeting
But we look at each other a lot
We smile at each other a lot
We whisper to each other and we lean on each
    other when we laugh
And knowing
Knowing for sure
That we can do this
That we could even
Even!
Hold hands
Here
Knowing
Knowing!
That we could be honest

That we could be us
Knowing that here
Here!
No one will make fun
No one will tease
No one will question or doubt or deny
Us
Who we are
What we are
Together
Knowing that
Knowing it all
Knowing it all for sure
Is the most beautiful feeling
I think I've ever felt
And Chloe looks really pretty today
And I can think that here
I could even
Say it
Here
And Chloe's nails are blue today
And Chloe still eats a banana every day and Chloe can still astound me with her magic
She can still say the alphabet backwards
She still
Writes the date
In gel pen
On her
Homework
She still has brown eyes

And I still
Notice them
I still notice
It all
And I know why
I am so
So sure
About why
And I
Love it
I love noticing
I love seeing
I love feeling
I love knowing
I love
Being me
I love being me
With her
I love

Being

Us

After the meeting
Somehow
We have to go back to class
We say goodbye to everyone
And people say goodbye to us
They use our names

And they smile
And say
See you next time
And oh oh oh
I cannot wait
For next time

I'm so scared of losing them

Why am I
Why did I
Why do I

We separate at the door
With smiles and looks of shock and joy
 and bewilderment
And we go
To class
And in class
Sitting
At the back of the room
Instead of in his seat
Next to mine
Is Andrew

He avoids my eye
He stares at his book
And all the joy
Starts to slip away from me
And I try my best
To cling to it
To keep it
To hold it
But Andrew
I need Andrew
He's my best friend
He's my oldest friend
And losing him
The idea of losing him
Makes
Me
Anxious
And
Scared
And
So
So
Sad

I don't know why I did it
I don't know why
When I walked into the
Classroom
My feet just
Kept
Moving
Past
My seat
Past
Her seat
Past
Our seats
I don't know
I don't understand

Why I

Did that

And when she
Walked in
And when she
Saw my empty seat
And when she
Scanned the room
And when
Her eyes
Locked onto mine

And when
I looked away
And when
And when
And when
Her eyes

My heart
My stomach
My skin
My bones

Break
Lurch
Hurt
Shake

Her eyes

I sit in my seat
Because I don't know what else to do
And I try to pay attention to maths class
But it's hard and it's confusing and I'm distracted and I feel
Silly and scared and
And did you know
That in July
Of 1947
In Roswell
New Mexico
Metal and rubber debris
Was found
That was thought to be
From a spaceship
Did you know
That?
I've read that it was a weather balloon
Not a spaceship
At all
But
There are people who think the
Weather balloon story
Was just a story
Was a cover-up
And I don't know
What I think
Because I don't know enough
Because there's so much
Conflicting

Information
And I hate that
Because I always
Always thought
There was true and there was false
Right and wrong
Real and fake
I thought the world made sense
But here I am
Happy and sad
At the same time
Confident and confused
I don't know if there were aliens in Roswell in 1947
I don't know if it was just a weather balloon
I don't know if there's life on Mars
And the worst part
Is that
I cannot
Know
Because the information
The true the right the real
Isn't there to be known
And I always
Always
Thought
That if I just learned
If I just knew
Everything
I would be safe and good and smart

But I never realised
How much there is
That just
Can`t
Be
Known
And right now
That is hitting me
In the stomach
Right in my middle
It is hitting me
Because one of the things
That just cannot be known
Right now
Is what is wrong
With Andrew

He runs out after class
And I try to follow
But our teacher calls me back
And reluctantly
I turn
And trot over to her
Stevie
She says
Yes Miss
I say
Are you OK?
She asks

You were very distracted during class
And I know you're having trouble
With some of the things we're covering
And I just want you to know
That yes
It's early days
But if you're already
Finding it tough
There is no
Absolutely no
Shame in accepting help
I know I know!
You are so smart and capable
I just want you to know
That if you need to join our extra after school lesson
That's OK
You just let me know
OK
I want you to excel and feel comfortable and confident in class
So you just feel free
To come to me
If you need help
Or you need guidance
Or you need
To join us after school

And I nod and I smile and I say thank you
And I leave

And I go to the bathroom
And I cry and I hold myself
And I try to breathe
In and out   in and out   in and out
And I wish I could go
To Andrew
Because he is very good
At helping me remember
How to breathe
Right
In and out
In hold out
In and out
But clearly
He wants nothing to do with me right now
And I don't know why
Or what I did
Or if I even did
Anything
Or how to
Fix it
How to make it all
OK
And I wish
I could go to Chloe
But she's in a different class
And she's probably with her new friends
And she thinks
I'm doing
So well

And I want her to think
I'm doing so well
And I don't want her to see me
Like this
Even though I know
She wouldn't
Judge me
I worry
That I
Would judge me
And I wish I could go to my mum
But she's at work and I'm at school and I'm OK now and I'm OK now and I'm OK now
And if I keep telling myself
Maybe it will be
True

I think about Dr Wells
About what she would tell me
She would help me breathe
She would tell me that everything my teacher said is right and true and real
It is OK
I don't have to know everything
I don't have to understand everything
I don't have to be the best at everything
I am good and kind and smart and worthy
I am good and kind and smart and worthy
I am good

And kind
And smart
And worthy
And I am OK
And I will be
OK
And the more I tell myself that
The closer I start to feel
To OK
I wipe the tears from my face
Splash it with water
I breathe and I breathe
And I go to my next class
Grateful for the five minute break
Grateful for Dr Wells
Grateful for my own
Strength
Andrew is at the back of the class again
And I am in my usual seat again
And he is staring at his book again
And I am trying to focus again
And then class is done
And he is gone again
And the day
Goes on
Just like
That

At home I wonder
If I should tell my mum
What my maths teacher said
But just the idea
Makes me blush with shame
No
No
I tell myself
No
There is no shame
But I can't help feeling it
I can tell myself there's no shame
I can believe that there's no shame
But what does it mean
When I just feel that shame
Anyway?
So I sit across from my mum
And I eat baked potatoes and too much cheese
And I say
Nothing

Mum tells me about her day
She tells me about work
About how well it's going
About the promotion she thinks she's about to get
She sounds so smart and sure

And I feel
So proud of her
I look at her
And I feel so lucky
And I feel so inspired
And I decide
Tomorrow
I will do so well in maths class
That no one will ever doubt me
Again

I do tell my mum about Andrew
I say that he's acting
Strange
That he's quiet
That he's avoiding me
And Mum says maybe
He just needs
Space
And that startles me
Space
Why would he need space?
Am I too much?
How much space does he need?
What if he needs
All the space
There is?
What if he never comes close
Again?

And Mum sees me
Start to spiral
A little
And she takes my hand
And she looks me in the eye
And she says
Hey
Hey
Stevie
Has Andrew ever
Hurt you?
Has he ever
Hurt your feelings
On purpose?
Has he ever
Abandoned you or made you feel
Silly or unwanted or unworthy
Has he ever
Done
Any of that?
And I don't even need a second to think
I just shake my head
No
No no and no
Never never never
Well then
My mum says
Why don't you just
Trust

Trust that he is doing what he is doing
For a reason
Trust that he will come around
When he is ready
Trust that he isn't being mean or doing this just
    to hurt you
Trust him
Trust your friendship
Trust Andrew

And I feel my eyes
Fill
And my hands
Shake a little
And my mum says
Oh
Oh Stevie
And she scoops me up
And she holds me
And she rocks me
And she soothes me
And I trust her
I trust her more than anyone
So I will listen
I will give Andrew his space
I will trust him
But I will still fight
For our
Friendship

Because it
Because he
Because we
Are worth fighting for
Even if right now
Fighting
Looks like taking a step back
Looks like space
Looks like time
I trust her
I trust myself
I trust him

The next day is a Saturday
Which means
It's a
Together day
Mum and me
We make pancakes
We do our chores
We watch movies
We cook dinner
We read
We talk we listen we learn
Together
Together
Together

Mum is still reading her space book
And she is still sharing
All the best bits with me
Did you know
She says
That the sun
Has been around for almost five billion years
And it's been burning
All that time
Without any real change
In temperature
Or brightness?
It's just been there
Burning bright
Which takes a
Phenomenal
Amount of energy
And stability and consistency
And I soak in that fact
And I file it away
And I say
Wow
And Mum smiles
And she puts a hand on my head
And she says
Doesn't that sound like you and Andrew
Doesn't that sound like your friendship
Long-lasting
Stable
Consistent

Phenomenal
The very brightest star
Doesn't that sound like you two?

And it does
It does
Andrew and I
Have been friends since we were babies
We've always been friends
When I get anxious I can rely on him to calm me
When I'm happy he laughs with me
When I told him I like like Chloe
He hugged me
And said
OK
Cool
And squeezed me tight
And I didn't need him
To say anything more
Than
OK
Cool
Because
He is Andrew
And I knew
What that
OK
Cool
Meant
It meant

I love you
You are my friend
And I support you
It meant
I am here for you
It meant
I am proud of you
I know that
Because I know him
And my mum is right
He is bright
Like the sun
And our friendship
Is bright like the sun
And the sun
Has been burning
Bright bright bright
For billions of years
So we can keep
Burning
Bright
For
As
Long
As
We
Want
To
And I know

I want
To
I just hope
No
I trust
That he does
Too

It's a Saturday
Which means
It's an alone day
My sister
Jessie
Has a match
So Dad left early
After planting a kiss on my head
And telling me to call for
Any reason
I make breakfast
Practise souffle pancakes
I do some homework
I'm finding science interesting
But
Overwhelming
Geography easy
But
Boring
Maths fun but
History cool but
But but but
There's always this feeling
Distracting me
Always the pull
To stare
At the
Back of
Her head

To try to
Read her
Thoughts
To try
To somehow
Send her a message
The message
To tell her
I'm sorry
I'm sorry
I'm sorry

I miss you and I'm sorry and I miss Chloe and I'm sorry and I miss you I miss you I miss you

I tidy my room
I tidy the kitchen
The sitting room
The bathroom
I change the sheets
Mine
Dad's
Not Jessie's
I do and I do
And still the day
Is only
Half done

My dad
Loves me
So much
But
But

My dad loves me so so much
My dad loves me
So so
Much

But

I'm the youngest
And I think
People think
That means I'm spoiled and
You know
The baby of the family

But I'm not

Dad had Jessie young
And for a while
It was just
The two of them
And then I
Well
Here I am

The baby of the family

And yes

I am loved

And yes

I have everything I need

But sometimes
Just
Sometimes
I feel
A little
Like I
Intruded
On their
Little life
Together
Jessie is a footballer
She plays for a pretty big team
And she's honestly

Really good

I used to want to be a footballer too
Like my sister
Like her

But
Well
Anyway
Because Jessie is away a lot
It's usually just me and Dad
And we have a really
Nice time together

He's a better baker
But I'm catching up

I'm pretty sure
Stevie
Is the smartest person I know

Chloe is the most talented

Jessie is the best footballer

Dad the best baker

So
Where does that leave me?

I do well at school
But not as well as Stevie

I'm talented at things
I suppose

But not like Chloe is
Not like that

I make great cookies
But Dad's are better
(to be honest)

And football
Football

I used
To love it
When Dad comes home
We eat dinner
I finish my homework
We watch tv
He falls asleep on the couch
I pop a blanket over him
I go to bed

That night I turn off all the lights
And look through my telescope
At the stars and the constellations and the moon
   and everything there is to see
Up there
I tell my alien
All about Andrew
And Chloe
And Rainbow Club
All about week one of school
About maths and how hard it is
Science and how interesting it is
English and how riveting it is
About all the people I met at Rainbow Club
Nate and Marie and Daire and Katie and everyone
   and everyone and everyone
About how they smiled at me
About how welcome I felt
And as I tell my alien
Somewhere out there in space
All about everything
I realise
How much good there was
And yes
The week had bad in it
Andrew's silence
His avoidance

The nerves
The maths
The panic
But there was also Andrew's cookies
Holding Chloe's hand
A day with my mum
Rainbow Club
Learning and growing and
Having my eyes
Opened
To so much
It was a big week
It was a
Big
Week
But I got through it
I enjoyed the good
I survived the bad
And next week
Next week
Can't come
Fast enough

Sunday is usually
Friends' day
We hang out
We play
We research
We bake
We eat
We are
Together

I don't know what to do
So I don't do
Much of anything
At all

At all
At all
At all
I miss them
I hope they know
They haven't done anything wrong
At all
At all
At all

On Monday morning
I meet Chloe at the gate
And she's worried
I tried to debate Andrew last night
She says
But he hung up on me
And I realised
She says
I haven't
Properly
Talked to him
In days
And I'm
Worried
She says

And suddenly I feel bad for not including Chloe more
For not telling her about Andrew
Sitting in a different seat
Running out of the classroom
Hiding
I should've told her
We are all
Best friends
But sometimes
I find that hard
To balance

I'm sorry
I tell her
And I tell her
Everything
Including what my mum said
And Chloe nods along and gasps and shakes
　her head
In all the right places
And then she says
OK
OK
OK
We
Will
Fix
This
But first
She says
We will go to class
And she hugs me
And says she'll see me at lunch
And we linger for a moment
Looking at each other
And just like that
We say even more to each other
With her eyes
Looking into mine
She says
That she loves Andrew too

Just like I do
She says that she is worried
But she knows it will be OK
She says that we will get him back
And I nod
And we part
And I feel
      Better

When Chloe and I
Became friends
I admit
I admit
I admit
I was
Worried

What if we didn't get along
Enough?
Weren't friendly
Enough?
Compatible
Enough?
What if I let Stevie
Down
Down
Down?

I was worried
That Chloe wouldn't like me
Enough
To be
Best
Friends
That I wouldn't like her
Enough
Though I already knew
I did
I thought she was cool

And
Interesting
And
Talented
And
I knew
Stevie
Liked her
Liked her liked her
Of course
So
Of course
There was pressure
Concern
Worry
What if what if
What if I lost Stevie?

And I know
It's silly
And ironic
I know
It's silly that
After everything
Worked out
And I came to love and be loved
By Chloe
The way I love and am loved
By Stevie
I know

It's silly
That now
I'm losing them both
And I know
It's silly
Ironic
Silly
That it's all
My own
Doing

I know
I just
Can't do
Anything
About it

I can't
Really

When Chloe and Andrew became friends
At first
I was a little
Nervous
That they would like each other
More than they like
Me
That they would be best friends
And wouldn't need me
And they did become best friends
But they did need me
They needed me to moderate the debates
They needed me to make them laugh when
 they argued
To show them how great they are
When they doubt it
To encourage them
When they're feeling shy
They need me
Because they love me
And I need them
I need Andrew to stay by my side
I need Chloe to hold my hand
I need them because I love them
And I know
I know
Need
Is a big word
And maybe we won't need each other for ever

But right now
With everything around us changing
We need each other
And if everything falls apart
If we drift apart
We will be OK
I will be sad
But I know
I know
I know
I know
I will be OK
And I know
No matter what
I will always be grateful
For them
So
When I walk into class
And Andrew is sitting at the back of the room
I give him space
I smile at him
And I wave
So he knows
I'm not mad
I'm not angry
I'm not hurt
So he knows
I'm still here
So he knows

He can come back
When he's ready
But still
Still I give him
Space

A smile
A wave
Just
A smile
A wave
Only
A smile
A wave
And suddenly
I feel

Lighter

Brighter

Loved
and
Loved
and
Loved

And

Trusted

I get through all my morning classes
Alone
The other kids in my class
Seem nice
But I don't know them yet
And I don't know if I have the energy or the space in my head
To work on making new friends in class right now
So I cut myself some slack
I show myself some grace
And I give myself time
I don't put pressure on myself
And I allow myself the space
I need
I am polite and I am friendly
But I know
There's no rush
There's no
Rush
I will make friends
When I am ready
And until then
I can be OK
Sitting here
By myself
I am OK
With myself

I eat lunch outside
Now
By the trees
And even though
Today
Is cold
I feel
Warm

A smile   a wave   a little bit   of hope

At lunch I sit with Chloe in the canteen and we eat and talk and plan
We talk about Rainbow Club and space and Sydney the octopus and our parents and her brother and school and books and mostly we talk about Andrew

But there isn't that much to say

Other than

Space

How much space?

How long do we wait?

And the truth is

We admit

We do not know

So we stop talking about Andrew

And we start talking

About

Nothing

Because I want to talk about

Maths

And how hard it is

And what my teacher said

But I can't

Because I'm

Embarrassed

And because Chloe

Thinks I am smart

And I need that

I need that

So we eat
And we are comfortable in our silence
And we just enjoy
Some time
Together
And I love this about our friendship relationship
   friendship

I love that we can just
Be

Just before maths class
I go into the bathroom
And I sit on the toilet and I close my eyes
And I whisper
To myself
Just to myself
You can do this
You are smart
You are brave
You are capable
You are smart
You are brave
You are capable
You are smart you are brave you are capable you are smart you are brave you are capable
You are   you are   you are
And I say it all
Over and over
Until I believe it
As much as I possibly can
Until I feel it
As strongly as I can
I say my affirmations
And I do some breathing exercises
And I go
To class

And I try
And I try
And I try
To learn
To keep up
To do well

But it is hard
It is so hard
It is confusing and it is complex and it makes no sense
To me
And I try
And I write my affirmations in the margins of my notes
And I breathe in and out   in and out
And I focus and I try
I try
I do
And sure
I don't panic
   Thank you affirmations
   Thank you breathing exercises
   Thank you me
But the maths
The numbers
The equations
They still don't make
Any sense

And I feel
Ridiculous
Silly
Useless
Hopeless

Hopeless

I try to tell my mum
I do
I try to tell her that maths is too hard
That I need help
That it's too much
But the words won't come out
I'm too disappointed in myself
I'm too ashamed
Cleverness is what I have
It's my thing
I know things
That's my *thing*
It's who I am
What I am
I am smart
I am clever
I am intelligent
I am
It's what I get the most praise for
It's what people say the most
So smart!

Wow!
So clever!
And right now
I don't feel very clever
And if I'm not as clever as I thought I was
As everyone else thought I was
Then what am I?

I try to tell my mum
I do
But I don't
I can't
I simply
Can't

I can't let her down

We have a test
A maths test
Just to see
How we're getting along
So far
The teacher says
And I could swear
Could swear
She looks at me
But I know
She probably didn't
It's probably just
Anxiety
Playing tricks
On me

She hands out the tests
Just one sheet of paper
Covered in little black printed numbers and
    symbols and I look at it and suddenly
My chest hurts
My tummy turns
My head feels dizzy
I take a deep breath
Deep down
Hold
Release

I try to silently let the air flow between my lips
I try to silently tell myself that I'm OK
I try to
Silently
Be OK
Be OK
Silent
In a silent room
Oh god
The room is so silent
Oh god
No it isn't
Because I can hear
Pencils
Scratching
I can hear answers being written
I can hear the clock ticking
And oh
Time is passing
Oh no
Time is passing
And I'm just sitting
I'm just
Sitting
Until I look up
And somehow
There's only a few minutes left
And I scribble numbers on the page
I try
I try

I do
I try
But I know
I know
I do
I know
None of them are
Right

When the tests are collected
We have a break
Just a couple of minutes between classes
And I go outside
For a few seconds
To breathe
To breathe and to try not to cry
And I fail
Again
I fail I fail I fail
Again again again

At the next Rainbow Club meeting
Chloe and I talk to someone named
Sage
Sage says their pronouns are she/they
She says we can use either
As both feel right
And I think
That's so cool
That their confidence is cool

Her self-assurance
I try to switch between pronouns
And it isn't the easiest thing
At first
But after a minute
I get used to it
Sage
She/they
Cool

We talk to a boy named Aaron
Who is gay
He has a boyfriend named Jake
And when he introduces us to him
They hold hands
Their hands find each other like magnets
And stick together
And fit together
And stay together
And I see Chloe
Glance at my hand
And I think
Maybe
Maybe soon
We could do that too
Not just on my couch
Or sitting on my bedroom floor
Not just when we're alone
Not just in some sort of secret

Maybe
Maybe soon

We decide to start the year off with a fundraiser
To start the year with goodness and kindness
We all throw out ideas
And land
Of course
On a bake sale
The best and biggest bake sale
You've ever seen
Of course
And
Of course
I immediately think
Of Andrew
Of how excited this would make him
How many ideas he would have
How he would offer to share recipes with everyone
Not his top secret ones
Of course
But really really good ones
How he would make the best cupcakes and cookies and
How he would be
So happy
And I wonder
Again
For the millionth time

Why he isn't
Here
With us
I share a look with Chloe
That lets me know
She's thinking the same thing and
Again
For the millionth time
I wonder
How much space
Is too much space

We've been sending out messages
For aliens
For a long time
We've sent out music and messages
Greetings and information and even whale sounds
We've sent them out into space
In the hope or fear that they'll be received

In 2006
The French Centre for National Space Studies
Sent out a TV show for aliens
They beamed it to a star called Errai
But because Errai is forty-five light years from us
It won't get there
Until 2051
But still
We try

We try to find life
To make connections
Even if it takes us years
Even if it seems pointless
Even if it seems hopeless
We try

I decide to try
With Andrew
To send out messages
Even if they won't reach him
Straight away
I sit one row closer during class
I slip recipes for cake pops and pies
and profiteroles
Into his locker   Oh! Recipes!
Then I sit one row closer the next day
And slip a playlist of our favourite songs
Into his locker   Oh! Our songs!

Then one row closer
A paper heart   Oh! A heart!

One row closer
A poem about friendship   Oh! A poem!

And then
Eventually   Oh!
I'm sitting next to him   Stevie!

I don't say anything
And neither does he
But it feels
Like progress
And though these days
Moving one step closer
Slowly
Slowly
Row by row
Inch by inch
Have been lonely
And sad
I feel
Hopeful
I have
Faith
I trust
                          Us

These last few days
Moving closer
Feeling closer

I have felt
So much
Less
Lonely
And so much
More
hopeful

But
When I get home
Jessie is outside
In the garden
Kicking
A ball
Against the wall
    Bang   bang   bang
Thump   thump   thump
Hey
She says
Wanna play?
    Bang   bang   bang
Thump   thump   thump

I go inside

Chloe comes over
We do homework
I say no thank you
To help with maths
So she won't see
How bad I am at it now
And she looks confused
But she smiles
And says OK
Mum makes us spaghetti
And the three of us eat together
And Mum and Chloe talk and talk
And I eat and I listen
And it makes me so happy
To see two people
Who mean so much to me
Get along
Get to know each other
To see them bond
To see them laugh and smile and exclaim together
It makes me feel
Warm and light and glowy
I love it
I love them

After dinner
Chloe and I

Curl up on the couch
We put on a music channel
And Mum lights the fire
Because it's started getting chilly
In the evenings
And the room is so warm
And so cosy
And I am so content
With Chloe by my side
And my mum singing in the kitchen
And Andrew
At least
Sitting beside me at school
Or I'm sitting beside him
I suppose
But it's enough
For me
For now
I feel good
I feel content
And then Chloe leaves
And Mum comes in
A piece of paper in her hand
And she says
Gently
Stevie
What is this?
What happened here?
And I look up
From my sleepy haze

And see my most recent maths test
In her hand
The bright red ink all over it
Declaring
Loudly
That I failed failed failed
I jump from the couch
And grab it from her
Nothing
I say
Nothing
It's nothing
And Mum says
Well clearly it's not nothing Stevie
Are you having trouble in class?
And I shout no before I'm even aware that I've
   opened my mouth
And she's surprised
Startled
Shocked
Stevie
She says
Softly
And I can't breathe
And she's looking at me
And she's worried
And I did that
And she's bound to be disappointed
And I did that

And she might be angry
And I did that
And she's looking at me with concern all over her face
And she's putting her hands on my shoulders
And she's guiding me to the couch
And I realise
I am panicking
I am not breathing properly
I am shaking
I am shivering
I can't swallow right
I feel sick
I am panicking
And I haven't panicked like this in a while
And Mum is in front of me
And she says
OK
OK Stevie
You know what to do
You are in control
You have the power
You can do this
In and out
In and out
Good
Good
In and out
And I'm crying
And Mum is making soothing noises

And telling me that I'm safe
And I know I am
But I don't feel it
I feel like there's danger all around me
I feel like I'm up in space
In the dark
And there's no air
I can't breathe
No matter how hard I try
Because there's no air to breathe
And I'm floating
And there's nothing to ground me
Nothing to hold on to
I'm up in space
And I don't like it
Then Mum says
STEVIE
And I snap back
And I'm on Earth
And there's a floor beneath my feet
And air surrounding me
And a cushion I can grab and hold close to me
  and touch and feel and know
It is real
And here is real
And I am real
And I am OK
And Mum kneels in front of me
And looks up at me

And she looks
Relieved
And I realise I'm breathing again
And things are starting to settle
And I'm starting to feel
Calmer

What's wrong Stevie?
My mum asks
And I whimper
Is higher maths too hard?
She asks
And I nod
And I wait
For her face to fall
For the disappointment to arrive
To pour down her face
But she just nods
OK
She says
Do you want grinds?
What feels best to you?
And I look at her
And I say
Um
I don't know
And she says
OK then
We'll have a think about it

Whatever you need Stevie
Whatever is best for you
That's what we'll do
And I don't know why I'm so surprised
Because my mum is good and kind and compassionate
She is caring and gentle
She would never
Never
Judge me
Like that
And I feel bad
Guilty
Awful
That I ever thought she would
And I tell her so
I say I'm sorry I'm so sorry I'm sorry
And she takes my hands
And she says
Stevie
You have anxiety
My love
There are things you know
And things anxiety tells you are true
And you are the smartest
Most aware
Most capable kid I know
But even you
Cannot possibly get it right
All the time
Sometimes that voice

The anxious voice
Will be loud
Louder than your voice
Maybe
Louder than mine
Maybe
But we just have to work on tuning out that voice
On talking back and saying no
I will be OK
I am safe
We just have to work on that
Me and you
And Dr Wells
We're working on it
But it will take time
And you cannot beat yourself up when you listen to that voice
It can be big
It can be loud
It can be convincing
Of course you'll believe it sometimes
But until you can silence or quieten it yourself
I am here
To tell you
You are OK
You are safe
You are home and you are loved
So so loved
Stevie
My Stevie

I cry again
But it's different
This time

Jessie
Is as good at football
As Chloe is at magic
Which means
She's so good
It baffles me
Impresses me
Inspires me

The difference
Though
Is that I don't love
Magic

I can watch Chloe
Learn and perfect and perform
And I think
Wow
How cool
How amazing
How lucky I am
That she shares this with me

                    But when Jessie
Practises   perfects   plays
I feel
Embarrassed
I feel
Humiliated

I feel ill
Remembering
Her face
When she told me
As I stood
In my gear
Ready
To try
To join
To   try
To   play
Just   to   play

Andrew
You can try
I guess
But
You're just
Never
Going to be
Very good

And I heard
The words
She left out

The unspoken
Like me
The silent

So really
What's the
Point?

And I should
Be really good
At the things I do
And the things I try
Shouldn't I?
Great baker
Great football player
Great at school
Great at friendship
Great son
Great brother
Great great great
But when I think about
That
I think
How could I possibly?
And if I'm being nice to myself
I think
How could I
When this is the best
I can do?
I am trying
My best
At least
But the rest of the time

I think
How could I
When I am not even good at being me?

After Jessie said
What she said
After she looked at me
Like I was
Pitiful
After she smiled and left the room

I quit
Playing
Watching
Caring

I quit
Talking about it
With Robert
My friend

I quit
Being Robert's
Friend

It was our thing
Our link
Our connection
It was the thing we shared the thing we had in
common it was our

Thing

And it hurt
And it made me sad
Because really
I wanted
I wanted

Nevermind

I quit
I miss them

We have a Rainbow Club meeting
And it's all hands on deck
To prepare for the bake sale
We have two days
We make lists of what everyone is making
So we don't have too much of the same things
We plan decorations
We make posters
We chat and we laugh and we have fun
And these people
These wonderful people
Are becoming friends
My friends
Our friends
And I feel so at home with them
Here
In this room
I feel so safe
So welcome
So seen and heard and appreciated
And I think
This group
Is changing things for me
I think
Just being here
Is making me braver

And more confident
Louder and brighter
More sure about who I am
Not that I doubted it
But it's nice to know
It's nice to know

Chloe and I say we'll make
Cookies
Chocolate chip
Of course
We've learned from the best
So surely
We can do it
We can make cookies
Just like his
Surely we can

After school Chloe and I walk home together
And I tell her
About maths
About how confusing it is
About how out of my depth I am
I tell her about how I didn't want her to know
I was finding it hard
In case she thought I wasn't smart
And she is
Aghast
Stevie!

She yells
Stopping in the middle of the path
And turning dramatically
You are the smartest person I know
If you were good at maths too
You would be far too powerful!
Please
Let me be the best at maths!
And please
Let me help
She looks at me hopefully
Pleadingly
And I say
Yes
Please
And she hugs me
A big bear hug
And says
Don't worry
I've got you

We work on maths all evening
And some things start to become a little clearer
Start to make
A little more sense
But mostly
I am just
Confused
All muddled
All puzzled

My brain feels like it's spinning
It feels tired and heavy and too full of numbers
Chloe
I groan eventually
Please
There's no use
It's no good
I can't do it
It's just too hard
And Chloe sighs
OK
She says
Then what do we do?
And I smile
And I tell her
I'll take extra lessons
After school
With other kids
Who feel like I do
And my mum comes out of nowhere to hug me
And Chloe joins us
And they tell me they're proud of me
For doing what's right for me
What's best for me
And that it's all all all
Good
The next day
I tell my maths teacher
That I'd like to join the maths after-school group
And she smiles

And says that sounds like a good plan
And that I'll do great in the group
She's sure of it
We go to the office together
And we get it all sorted
And I don't feel ashamed
Or embarrassed
Or disappointed
I feel proud of myself
For doing what I need to do
For knowing what's right for me
For not putting myself in a situation
That would just make me feel
All those horrible feelings
I feel hopeful
I feel excited for my new group
I feel great

In English
I make a joke
About Shakespeare
And Andrew
Beside me
Lets out a tiny snort
And oh
It's such a good day

I met them
Nate
I was leaving school late
Trudging down the hall
My bag making my shoulders
Ache
So full I had to carry some of my notebooks
In my hands
And there they were
Nate
Walking towards me
And of course
I put my head down
Like a coward
And of course
I sped up
Like a coward
And of course
I dropped my notebooks
And of course
And there they were
Immediately
Helping me
Picking up my books
Making a silly joke about getting stuck on the floor
With a bag so big
Something about a turtle on their back
And they're so right
That's so

Exactly
How I feel
That
Even though Nate was joking
I burst into tears

And it's all so silly
So ridiculous
So like a scene
In some cheesy
Cheesy movie
That I cry harder
And Nate is so nice
So gentle
Speaking so softly
Asking politely before putting a hand
On my shoulder
Sweetly reminding me
To breathe
Saying sorry
Even though they did
Nothing wrong

I sniffle
And I snot
And I cry and I cry and I cry
And the whole time
Nate is there
They are there
And we sit on the floor

Like we're waiting for cookies
And after a while
I let out a little laugh
And Nate looks at me
Kindness in their eyes
Mixed with
Curiosity
They smile a little
Raising their eyebrow
In an unspoken question
And I look down
And I say
Your group sounds cool
And they say
You should join then
And I say
I can't
I'm not
I don't think
I don't know if I'm
And
I know
Allies are welcome...
And Nate nods along
And says
Allies are welcome
Totally welcome
But that doesn't feel
Totally truthful
Either

Does it?
And I shake my head
And I might cry again
I try not to
But I might
So instead
I just
Ramble
I talk fast fast fast
Because
Nothing fits exactly
Right
Which means
I don't fit exactly right
Nothing feels exactly right
Which means
I don't feel exactly right
Nothing is exactly right
So
So
So

A hand on my shoulder again
A little squeeze
And I turn
And Nate says
You are
Exactly right
For right
Now

You don't need to know
Everything
None of us do

And that surprises me
Because they seem
To have it all figured out
But
I say
You know
Who you are and who
Who
You
Like

And Nate
They turn to me fully
So we're face to face
And they look me in the eyes
And they say

Who you like
Isn't who you are
It's a part of you
Just a part
Not the whole of you
Not the
Whole
Of you
You are so much

You are the things you like and the people you
Love and hate and look up to
You are your opinions and your thoughts and
Your feelings
All of them
You are every experience you've ever had
The good the bad the weird
Everything you're good at and everything
You suck at
You're your favourite superhero and
Your favourite song
The silly inside jokes that make you laugh
The most embarrassing moments and the
Coolest ones
You are everything
All at once
You are so much
More
Than
You
Think
You
Are

And they seem so wise
So much older than the sixth year they are
That it almost makes me sad
For a second
Then they smile
And their smile

Is the smile of a kid
Just like me
So I smile back
And I take a deep breath
And I ask
Because I know they'll answer

What do I do?

And Nate
Nate says
You go home
And you look around your room
At all the proof of you
Drawings you drew
Poems you wrote
Notes that make no sense to anyone
But you and your friends
A football under the bed
A teddy you can't get rid of
Socks on the floor
You look at it all
All the undeniable proof of you
And you think
I am more
Than even
This
I am so
Much
And I will be

Even more
I just need
To let
Myself

And I ask
If I can hug them
And they say yes
And we hug
And we walk out of the school together
And they say goodbye
And I close my eyes
And I feel the sun on my skin
The breeze in my hair
I feel my body
Holding me up
Moving me forward
I feel my mind
Whirring
With all of these new possibilities
I feel my face
Break into a smile

Chloe and I are in the kitchen
Surrounded by ingredients
Peering down at a recipe
How does he do this?
We say together
So many instructions
I say
So many ingredients
She says
So much mess
My mum says

We begin
And immediately
We are covered in flour
There is butter underneath my nails
And I am disgusted
Chloe has sugar in her hair
And she is oblivious
Mum has left the kitchen

Our first attempt at dough is too sticky
The second too crumbly
And when we eventually try to actually bake
    the cookies
They turn into one giant paper-thin cookie
When we taste it
We both gag and cough a little
This is not going to plan

Andrew
Always made it look so easy
He'd breeze in
Arrange his ingredients neatly
Whip up some dough in no time at all
And have the kitchen spotless by the time his perfect
Always perfect
Cookies were ready

I can tell
That Chloe is thinking about him too
But there's something else on our minds as well
So we start with that
What do we do?
She sighs
We promised to bring cookies
It's our first event with the Rainbow Club
We can't let them down
I take her hand
We'll figure it out
I tell her
Maybe more sugar?
Less butter?
Another egg?
We are smart and capable
We have to be able to make cookies!
But she shakes her head
And when she looks at me
There are tears in her eyes

I miss him
She says
I miss debating with him
And playing games with him
And even doing homework with him
I miss the smell of cookies and the sound of his
 laugh
I miss his jokes and his facts and his face when
 I did that trick with the sticks
Where there's three and then—

Five
I say
He loves that one
She rests her head on my shoulder
And sniffles a little
And I make up my mind
Right then
To do not just what's right for me
But what's right
For all of us

The phone rings three times
Before his dad answers
Hi
I say loudly
It's Stevie
Is Andrew there?
And his dad lets out a big sigh
And says oh Stevie
Thank goodness
We've missed you
He's just upstairs

I tell Andrew's dad everything
All the way up to our baking debacle
And he says
Well
I know exactly what to do
I'll see you soon
Thanks Stevie
And we hang up
Twenty minutes later
Twenty tense minutes later
The doorbell rings
And we jump
And we run
And there
Is Andrew

And he looks at us
And he smiles
A tiny smile
And he says
My dad says you tried to bake
Now why would you do that
Without
Me?
And I want to run and jump and hug him
But I hold it in
He looks shy and reserved
And unsure
But he is here
He is
Here
    And that's enough for now

I think
Maybe
Part of knowing yourself
Is letting yourself
Be known

I think
Maybe
Keeping my best friends
So far from me
Feels like
Keeping me
From myself
From knowing
And understanding
Myself
Because maybe
It is

I think
Maybe
I see this group
They're part of
This group
Of people
Kids
Like us
Who know
How they feel
And what they think

And what
No
Who
They
Like
And I think I
Feel this
Pressure
To be the same
To know
But I don't
I thought I did
I thought
At least
I had an idea
But I've only ever liked
Like liked
One person
Ever
One person
No
One
Boy

And I think
I liked being friends
I liked sharing a connection
I liked having something in common
With someone nice
I liked having a safe place to like what I liked

And I think
I see Stevie
And Chloe
And Stevie and Chloe
And I know
That
Is liking someone
And I don't know
That I've ever felt that
That I ever will
That I ever want to
It's all just
Maybe maybe maybe
And maybe
That's OK
Because
I think
No
I know
Right now
I'm happy
I'm happiest
Being a friend
Being their friend
So I think
No
I know
I should just
Let myself

Andrew takes one look at our mess
And rolls his eyes
How about
This time
I show you how it's done
He says
And Chloe and I look at each other in shock
You would share your recipe with us?
We ask
And he just nods
And looks down
And says
Yeah
Of course
Really quietly
And we nod and say
Yes
Yes please
And together
We make cookies

When the perfect cookies are in the oven
And the piggy timer is set
And the sweet smell is filling the kitchen
And the mess is cleared away
We sit on the floor
So Andrew can watch his cookies
Our cookies

I take a deep breath
Andy
I start
But he interrupts
It's the club
He says
The LGBTQIA+ club
The Rainbow Club
That's the problem

And hearing him say those words
My Andrew
About my club
My friends
My people
It hurts my heart

What do you mean?
Chloe asks
And Andrew looks at her
And he begins

I wanted to join too
He says
And Chloe immediately interrupts
Why didn't you?
You could have!
You should have!
And he looks at her

And she stops
And he says
I couldn't
I can't
You two
You know who you are
How you identify
Who you
Like
Like like
You're both so sure of yourselves
So confident
So
So
So brave

He's getting teary now
So we each offer one of our hands
Just in case
And he takes them both
Holds them tight

He's quiet for a minute
So I slowly
Gently
Say
Andrew
Are you saying
Are you

And he looks at me
And he shakes his head
Then he nods
Then he shakes his head again
Then he huffs out a breath and says
I don't know!
That's the problem!
You two know
You know for sure
And I just
Don't
You can join that group and introduce yourselves
And say exactly who you are
And know
You belong
There
I can't
I can't

And we squeeze his hands
And we look at each other
And Chloe nods at me
And I say

Andy
You don't need to know anything
We're thirteen
We don't need to be sure of anything
We just need to feel

That's all we need to do
All I am sure of is how I feel about Chloe
I know that's true because I feel it
So so strongly
But it took me a while and an adventure and
   a nice librarian and a lot of doubt and worry
   and bravery
To get to that place
But I'm still figuring out what it all means

I'm not
Chloe says
I'm gay
Lesbian
For sure
I've known a long time
And I'm sure
I know it and I love it and I'm proud of it
And I'm not saying it to make you feel bad
Andy
I'm saying it because I think it shows
That this
Is different for everyone
And your discovery
Your exploration
Your adventure
Can be whatever you want it to be
Or need it to be
Even if you're thirty or something

And you still don't know
That's still OK
You can take your time

I look at her
And I feel my heart grow
And I look at him
And I feel it surge
With sympathy

Oh Andy
I say
Can I hug you?
And he nods
And he sniffles
And we hug
And he says
But I still
Can't join the club
And I say
Silly
Of course you can
It isn't about knowing everything
Or understanding everything
Even yourself
It's about friendship
It's about having a safe place
To figure it all out
You
Andrew

Are more than welcome
And he cries
And he shakes
And we hold him
And we comfort him
And we tell him
That he is Andrew
And that is enough
That in time
Things will make more sense
And that we will be right there
Holding his hands
And helping him through
And some day
He might like like someone too
And no matter who they are
We can't wait
To meet them
But mostly
Above all else
We think he
Is the very
Very
Best

The cookies are perfect
Of course
And they sell out first
And everyone
Gathers around
Andrew
And thanks him and compliments him
And my chest swells
As I watch him blush
And smile
As we're standing
At our nearly empty table
With just crumbs and the odd cupcake left
I think of something
A question
Hey
Andrew
I say
And he looks at me
And I take a deep breath and ask
What did your dad say to convince you to come to my house?
What did it take?
And he smiles at me
And he says
He just told me you needed me
That's all it took

Of course that's all it took
We look at each other
And so much passes between us
And I know
I know for sure
Mum was right
I was right
To trust
Andrew

After the bake sale
We have a meeting
And Andrew sits next to me
And looks at me nervously
Then
When Nate says
Well
Looks like we have some new faces
Would you like to introduce yourselves
Andrew tenses
And I worry
As we listen to a girl named Willow introduce herself
And say she is bisexual
Her pronouns are she/her
And she's so happy to be here
I wonder
What Andrew
Is going to say
Then
He stands

And he smiles
And he says

Hi
I am Andrew
And that's all I know for sure right now!

Everyone beams at him
Everyone nods
And Nate says
Welcome Andrew
We're happy to have you!

And Andy
Andy falls back into his seat
Relief pouring off him
Then he straightens
And he sits up tall
And he looks around the room
And I watch him
Take it all in
So many people
In this one little room
People of different genders and races and religions
People with different identities
People who welcome him and accept him
And all he is
Even if he doesn't know
All he is

Just yet
Here
He is safe
And I can see that hit him
I can see him
Relax
I can see his chin rise and his shoulders loosen
I can see my friend
My best friend
Begin to feel
At peace
And it is
Beautiful

During the meeting
Andy joins in on conversation
He comes up with ideas for our next fundraiser
He makes jokes that make everyone
Everyone!
Laugh
He is
Himself
Again
At last
And I look at Chloe
And I see her watching him too
And she catches my eye
And she smiles shyly
Which is odd for Chloe

She is not shy
But then her eyes flick down to my hand
And I understand why
And I decide
To let her be the shy one
This time
And I reach down
And I take
Her hand

No one says anything
The meeting continues
But I see people notice
Willow grins
Nate looks right at me and mouths
I knew it
Which makes me laugh
Marie puts her hand on her heart and smiles smiles smiles
But really
Everything
Just
Carries
On
And I am holding Chloe's hand
And she is holding mine
And Andrew is talking loudly and bravely and making everyone giggle and
I love my friends
Andrew

Chloe
Rainbow Club
I love them
And I love myself
And all I am
I am brave and I am strong and I am vulnerable
I am kind and I am a good friend and daughter and person
I am smart even if I don't know everything
But I am so much more than just smart
I am so much
I am so
So much

And today
Right now
In this moment
I feel so proud
I feel
So
Proud

I've already eaten
Almost half of my popcorn
By the time he arrives
The movie is about to start
The trailers are over
My heart is starting to feel
Heavy
But I tell it
Heart
We will be
OK
No matter
What
For now
Let's just have
A little
Hope
And then
Someone plops an extra large drink
Into the holder beside me
Whispers
Hey Andy
And drops into the seat

And my heart
    Relaxes
And I smile
And I say
Hey Robert

ABOUT THE AUTHOR

Meg Grehan is the author of five novels-in-verse, they are *The Space Between*, *The Deepest Breath*, *Baby Teeth*, *The Lonely Book* and *The Brightest Star* (May 2025). Her books have won two Children's Books Ireland Awards and been nominated for the Waterstones Children's Book Prize, An Post Irish Book Awards and the Yoto Carnegie Medal for Writing

She lives in County Donegal in the north-west of Ireland where she spends her time writing, reading poetry and hugging trees.

ABOUT *THE DEEPEST BREATH*

There is so much that Stevie doesn't know. She doesn't know about all the fish in the sea. She doesn't know all the constellations of the stars. And she doesn't know why she feels this way about Chloe.

A Bank Street Best Children's Book of 2022 with Outstanding Merit

A Booklist 2021 Editor's Choice

Winner: Judge's Special Prize, Children's Books Ireland Awards 2021

Shortlisted: Waterstones Children's Book Prize 2020

We hope you have enjoyed reading *The Brightest Star*. The following few pages will introduce you to some other books published by Little Island that you might also like to read.

The Lonely Book
By Meg Grehan

We are a family
Perfectly formed
We are honest and open and ourselves
We are together together together
We are made of love

Annie loves helping out in her moms' bookshop. But she knows something is troubling her older sibling, and her moms are worried too. Even the bookshop is upset.

The Wordsmith
By Patricia Forde

How many words do you need to survive? "Love", "hope", "freedom" – in the dystopian future of Ark, after a climate change disaster, these words are being banned. One girl takes a stand against this loss of language – she is the Wordsmith.

Mother Tongue
By Patricia Forde

After global warming came the Melting.
Then came Ark.

The new dictator of Ark wants to silence speech for ever. But Letta is the wordsmith, tasked with keeping words alive. Out in the woods, she and the rebels secretly teach children language, music and art.

Now there are rumours that babies are going missing. When Letta makes a horrifying discovery, she has to find a way to save the children of Ark – even if it is at the cost of her own life.

The Girl Who Fell To Earth
By Patricia Forde

Nobody can ever know Aria's secret: she has human DNA.

Raised on Planet Terros, Aria was taught to hate humans and their destructive ways.

But when she is sent to release a deadly virus and end the failed human experiment, Aria realises everything she thought she knew about Earth was a lie.

The mission goes wrong. And now dark forces from Aria's past are out to destroy her.

The Wolfstongue Saga

By Sam Thompson

Prepare to enter the hidden world of the Forest in the Wolfstongue Saga.

"We had a name for a certain human child. This was the child who would walk side by side with the wolves and know our silence. The child would be our voice. So that we could live as wolves ought to live. Free from words. The name for that child was: Wolfstongue."

Run for your Life

By Jane Mitchell

Anzari and her mother fled for their lives to Ireland, where they live in a bleak Direct Provision centre. They long for their own hot, vibrant country. But to go back would mean certain death.

When Azari runs, she feels strong and free. But Azari has secrets — and she's still running for her life.

ABOUT LITTLE ISLAND

Little Island is an award-winning independent Irish publisher of books for young readers, founded in 2010 by Ireland's first Laureate na nÓg (children's laureate), Siobhán Parkinson. Little Island books are found throughout Ireland, the UK, North America, and in translation around the world.

You can find out more at littleisland.ie

RECENT AWARDS FOR LITTLE ISLAND

Highly Commended: British Book Awards Small Press of the Year 2024

Youth Libraries Group (UK) Publisher of the Year 2023

IBBY Honour List 2024
The Táin by Alan Titley, illus. by Eoin Coveney
Things I Know by Helena Close

An Post Irish Book Awards: Teen and YA Book of the Year 2023; Shortlisted: British Book Awards 2024
Black and Irish: Legends, Trailblazers & Everyday Heroes by Leon Diop and Briana Fitzsimons, illus. by Jessica Louis

An Post Irish Book Awards: Children's Book of the Year (Senior) 2023
I Am the Wind: Irish Poems for Children Everywhere ed. by Sarah Webb and Lucinda Jacob, illus. by Ashwin Chacko

White Raven Award 2023; Shortlisted: Carnegie Medal for Writing 2023; Shortlisted: YA Book Prize 2023; Finalist: Kirkus Prize 2023
The Eternal Return of Clara Hart by Louise Finch